Colonial Adventure
and
Other Stories

Ann Ackroyd.

Colonial Adventure and Other Stories

H. Ann Ackroyd

Copyright © 2011 by H. Ann Ackroyd.

Library of Congress Control Number: 2011904226
ISBN: Hardcover   978-1-4568-8138-2
               Softcover   978-1-4568-8137-5
               Ebook   978-1-4568-8139-9

All rights reserved. No part of this book may be reproduced or transmitted in any form or by any means, electronic or mechanical, including photocopying, recording, or by any information storage and retrieval system, without permission in writing from the copyright owner.

This book was printed in the United States of America.

To order additional copies of this book, contact:
Xlibris Corporation
1-888-795-4274
www.Xlibris.com
Orders@Xlibris.com
95299

Contents

Colonial Adventure 7-118

Haitian Girl 119-129

Actor 130-135

Truncated 136-145

Persian Rug 146-148

The Veil 149-151

Simba Kubwa Speaks... 152-154

Colonial Adventure

Prologue

In the year 1936
two young sophisticates
Margaret and Blair
peeled themselves away from London's social scene
heading for Thomas Cook
where a man in morning suit
recognised their kind immediately.
He'd seen it all before
that sense of entitlement
that need for space,
"So it's Africa," he said without preliminary.
"East coast or west coast?"

As fiends on the dance floor
Margaret and Blair packed first a gramophone
then, because standards must be upheld,
other essentials
crystal glass, embroidered jacket and chenille gown
along with tropical gear
of long-threaded Egyptian cotton
and capacious pockets.

At Sea

At the docks in Southampton
amidst shouting, waving, streamer and bunting
sailors hauled in the hawsers
retrieved the gangplank.
Whistles blew, foghorn sounded
the mighty liner, pilot now aboard
drifted from the dock
red ensign aflutter
into the Solent.
Britain was off again
to colonize the globe.
On board, at the railing
Margaret and Blair
stood glass in hand
drinking toasts to family and friends
on the docks below.
He kept an elegant arm draped over her shoulders
as tugs steered the vessel
past warehouse and upturned face
downstream on this first leg
of a life-defining adventure.

Cold bright air pinching their cheeks
two lone figures sat on deck
wrapped in blankets.
The tang of salt, sea and fish
filled their nostrils
while gulls screeched overhead
and wind ripped at the ensign.
They passed the Isle of Wight and on to open water

leaving Britain behind.
"It'll be warmer in Africa" said Blair
as they folded their blankets
and stored away chairs.
"Not too hot either, or so we hope," replied Margaret
for they had chosen wisely
buying land although within the tropics
on the high veld and therefore mild.

On the Bay of Biscay
they withstood storm and high sea.
Off Madeira they watched children dive
for silver in crystalline waters.
Consummate ballroom dancers
they partied through the nights
to the rhythms of samba, fox-trot and rumba
always to an audience
always to applause
for they were indeed a handsome pair
he with the looks of a matinee idol
she green-eyed with black-hair.
Then came the time to toast Table Mountain
with Scotch
they were tired of champagne
tired of luxury, extravagance, frivolity
they wanted to get on with the job.

The Train

took them on trundling trek
first north-west to Mafeking
Kimberly on the left
diamonds
the Witwatersrand on the right
gold
where the vultures had already gathered
already feasted.
Margaret and Blair however
continued on the tracks
along the eastern edge of the Kalahari
to Francistown and into Rhodesia.
The pace was leisurely
with many stops for passengers to ramble
and hunters to feed them.
From the train windows
and the platforms behind each carriage
Blair and Margaret were often treated to stunning spectacles
of wildebeest, giraffe, buffalo and zebra
stretching in full gallop across the savanna.
"I long to ride with them" said Margaret
green eyes flashing.
"And so you shall, my love," said Blair
wondering, as so often
at the wild and untamed spirit of this person
with slender neck,
pixie face and jet black hair.

In spite of their impatience
the long journey
offered countless occasion
to pick the brains of fellow passengers.
"Tell us about the Shona
their language, their habits, their housing, their food.
How do we go about acquiring
horse, cattle and fish?
How to hire
carpenters, drivers and orderlies?
Accountants, servants, builders and cooks?
Tell us, please!"

Preparations

In Salisbury,
capital of Southern Rhodesia
armed with letters of introduction, addresses, recommendations
they visited all manner of ventures
listened to advice, spoke to officials, studied equipment.
Then they headed east to Gomboli
ten thousand pristine acres
within the tropics
but sufficiently high
for the air to be cooler and dry.

Gomboli

On their first day
Blair
with the aid of a factotum
mustered a work force
from those offering their services.
The ones he accepted—he accepted most all—
started right away
erecting for themselves
rondavels of pole 'n dagga[1]
thatched with tall savanna grass
and floored with hardened cow dung.

On that self-same day
Margaret crawled out of bed at dawn
saddled her borrowed mare
—their own mounts were still en route from Capetown—
galloped into the plains
amongst kopjies[2] of granite
and massive mounds made by busy ants.
It bothered her that she disturbed the herds
ostrich, sable, eland, kudu
that galloped away long before she could reach them.
Life in Africa would not always be the way she planned.

---

[1] Pole and mud
[2] Granite piles (singular kopjie or kopje))

In whirlwind activity
the couple slaved from dawn to dusk
on horseback
in lorry, ox cart
tractor
whatever served
supervising
building, clearing
planting
tobacco, cotton, mealies[3]
and in frost-protected areas
fruit trees
mango, papaya, avocados, lychee.
They built
barn, shed, store, stable, silo
dairy and pigsties
along with dips against ticks
for the native cattle which
together with dogs that Blair used for hunting
they'd bought locally.
Blair referred to the latter as
"Egyptian whippets, all rib and prick,"
regardless of what they ate
they remained emaciated.
As personal pets
the couple brought in from Britain
three Great Danes of impressive pedigree
each as big as a pony.

---

[3] Corn

At dusk
the couple came home to the house on the kopje
walls of granite
with steps that swept in a gentle arc
away from a door of teak.
After wallowing in warm baths
then changing from cotton and khaki
into finest wool and shantung
they'd sip Scotch by the pool and dine from silver salver.
Standards must be observed
regardless.

Hidden Lives

One evening Blair lounged in long-limbed elegance
on the steps with Margaret at his side
blowing perfect smoke rings into the star-studded night.
Suddenly from the land below
desperate screams pierced the silence
followed by splutters and gurgles.
Margaret jumped to her feet
"What's that?"
"Don't worry, just dinner for a family that needs it."
Blair spoke of a leopard with cubs
living in a den on a neighbouring kopjie.
"That was a person," said Margaret.
"No, not person, bobbejaan[4]. They're destructive bastards!
Earlier
I saw a troop near her lair
foraging."
Margaret sighed,
"Africa," she said, "so violent and messy
enough to spoil dinner
for me if not leopards."
"We can't have that," said Blair taking her arm
escorting her inside
for their own less gory dining.

---

[4]   . . . baboon

Blair

At weekends Blair and Margaret
threw parties for house-guests from Salisbury.
As always they danced to the gramophone
feasted with silver and crystal
played tennis and ping-pong
swam.
"I understand now, Blair," commented a visiting dignitary,
"why you don't hanker for home."
He meant Britain
as did most white Rhodesians using the word.
Blair felt he was under attack
became defensive,
"We maintain standards
go home often
do what we did before
attend party, show, gallery, shop.
We're English not African.
We haven't gone native."
"So" said the man. "You'd fight for your country?"
He arched an eyebrow in query.
Outrageous!
"Of course!" said Blair
"How could you doubt it?"

The year was 1939
Blair joined up, was commissioned
marched with the army north
chasing Italians from Abyssinia and Somalia.
Stationed in Eygpt
they fought Jerry
then witnessed the end of Fascism
Mussolini
dangling by his feet at a gas station.
In all those years Blair never came home
not once.

Margaret

Although pregnant when Blair left
—Morgan was on his way—
Margaret ran Gomboli spending the days as before
in truck or on horseback
checking on gangs
workshops, transport, stables
constructing, planting, tending
crop, fishpond, poultry, vegetables,
dairy
beef-herds of Aberdeen Angus
even goats,
but these didn't last
after a rambunctious ram
spotted his own image in the gloss of her Studebaker
and butted it
with enthusiasm and repeatedly.
The farm was a commercial enterprise
run for private gain
but also feeding the country, providing export, supporting empire and
ally.

Born into the habits of command
Margaret's managerial activity came naturally
as much part of her
as her flashing green eyes and slender neck.
As the product of a long line of empire builders,
India, Kenya, Carribean, Sudan.
Portraits of these worthies
mustachioed and weighted with medal
glared at her
throughout childhood
from the walls of her ancestral home.

In running Gomboli
she had a legion of minions
black and white to guide and assist
yet she was always in charge and like most of her kind
harsh with the intransigent while just with those who complied:
school, clinic, housing, food, pay
all generous by standards of the day.

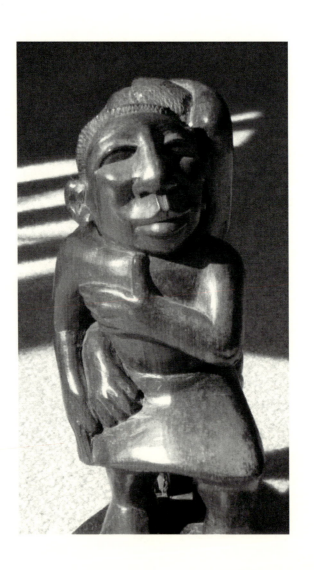

Nanny Lovely Speaks

Och-Poor-Wee-Mite was shrieking again
Nanny Lovely couldn't bear to hear a child cry.
Her sculpted lips
lifted at the corners and given to laughter
puckered in worry.
Where was Nanny Scotland?
She should be attending her duty.
She, who came from Britain,
supposedly trained to raise babies,
was letting Och-Poor-Wee-Mite starve.
Ridiculous!
Bottles!
Formulas!
What was wrong with a woman's breast?
The effervescence of Nanny's bounteous nature
couldn't resist the absurdity.
She erupted into the laughter stored
ever-ready
in rounded cheeks.
Then she remembered Och-Poor-Wee-Mite
victim of this folly
wiped away the mirth, stuck out her chin and entered the nursery.

Nurture

Fearless
she picked up the screaming bundle
crooning sweet nothings in Shona
held him to her chest.
He quietened, tried to suckle
so she settled on a chair
pulled aside her bib
unbuttoned her blouse
and offered him the abundance of her breast.
Looking down at the fair head on her dark skin
she noticed how different the image
to similar sessions with Isaac
yet the noisy sucks, slurps and burps
were the same
as too
her sense fulfilment, for she knew
with her god-given riches
she nurtured
not only Och-Poor-Wee-Mite
but Africa, the world and the future too.

At mission school
Nanny learnt that Christianity's exhortation to love
suited her nature.
No vendettas, violence or resentments for Nanny Lovely
not even toward Nanny S.
As Nanny sat nursing Och-Poor-Wee-Mite
she sang the songs of her people
those she sang to her sons, Norbert and Isaac,
the same songs her parents and grandparents sang
might now be doing at this very moment with her boys.

How lucky to be black
to be part of a community
sisters, aunts, cousins, grandparents
all happy to have youngsters to nurture!
She'd hate to be white
living in a house on a kopjie
ruling the roost
isolated
without love or affection.
Thus she often said
Och-Poor-Wee-White instead of Och-Poor-Wee-Mite.

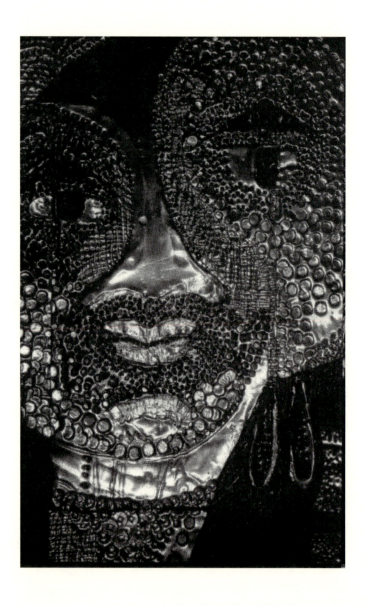

Explosion

When Nanny Scotland entered
laden with a tray of laundered nappies
the first thing that caught her eye
was a little white head
as delicate as a frangipani
nestled in the gleaming black of Nanny L's all engulfing breast.
She dropped her load
shrieked,
"Filthy black umfazi[5]!
What are you doing?
He's not your piccannin, he's white.
Give him to me!"
Nanny Lovely got to her feet
turned, buttoned her blouse and straightened her bib.
Nanny Scotland
clawing at her back, screeched,
"Give me that child!"
while Morgan added to the upheaval
bellowing in ear-splitting rage.
He had healthy lungs for one so young.

---

[5] Black woman

Everyone in the house came running
Margaret too
she'd been at breakfast in the dining room.
The tableau froze as she stood in the nursery door
dressed for riding
in high boot and jodhpur.
"What's happening?" she demanded, green eyes flashing.
Nanny Scotland hysterical and weeping
babbled
"That horrible dirty black umfazi . . .,"
sob, sniff, gulp.
Margaret, at her authoritarian best, didn't allow her to finish,
"Stop right there, Miss McAllen!.
I won't hear another word against Nanny Lovely."
She glared at the snivelling wreck
while renewed crescendo from Morgan
required she stop, block her ears, wait
before saying,

"Nor will I endure such behaviour
you've badly upset the child
obviously the job doesn't suit you."
"But she . . ." Nanny Scotland began.
Margaret cut her off,
"You'll pack your bags, a driver will take you to Salisbury.
Compensation will be adequate."
Nanny Scotland
nose and eyes streaming, mouth a contorted cavity
stammered a few more words
before Margaret hustled her out saying,
"Nanny Lovely, take Master Morgan to the garden
calm him.
You do it better than I."

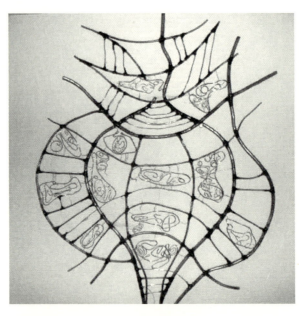

Garden

Nanny Lovely
clasping Och-Poor-Wee-Mite to her chest
descended the steps
headed for the pool where a shelter with a low front wall
looked out over the veld
to river, ant-hill and neighbouring kopjie.
She heard the birds
the cry of a battleur
—saw him circling—
heard the "go-away" bird, guinea fowl and hoopoo
all pleasantly soothing
after the fortissimo renderings
from Nanny S and the child.
Nanny L had to admit
unwillingly
despite formula and bottle
Morgan had no problem
retaining the assertiveness common to whites!
Fortunately he now slept
allowing Nanny to hear the Studebaker
crunching on driveway gravel
coming to remove the intruder.
Luckless woman. Nanny bore no grudge
but it was right she should go
right for Och PoorWee Mite
right because someone who didn't like blacks
shouldn't be in Africa.
How could Nanny S say Nanny L was dirty?
That wasn't possible where Margaret prevailed!

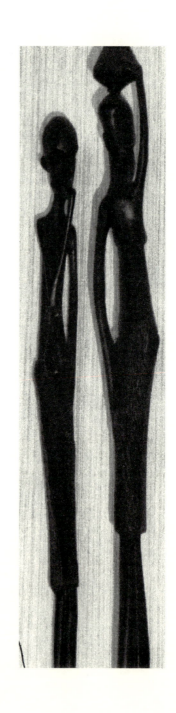

She who insisted on clean clothing daily
on toilet paper by the ream
on hand washing
again and again and again
constant showers
soap, soap, soap
scrubbing, disinfectant, pumice stone, tooth brush.
Strange that blacks hadn't turned white from such exaggerated ablutions!
Not that Nanny didn't enjoy being clean
she did
but wished those in the compound had it as easy.
Yet if they did
she'd miss the times with friends at the river
fun, laughter, splashing
cleaning their teeth with ashes, till they gleamed in the sun
laundering with blue mottled soap
scrubbing with pebbles
laying out clothes to dry on the rocks.
And the conversations! The laughter!
Nanny smiled recalling the hilarity
at her tales of life in the house on the kopjie.
A favourite was Nanny's description
of underwear worn by white women
insight gained from Nanny's job
of washing by hand
the more intimate items of Margaret's apparel
each described in abundance of detail
suspender belt, bra, panty, petticoat, nightie, stocking
all from Britain and not easily imaginable
for exuberant African bodies.

Morgan

An early memory for Morgan was his mother on horseback
wielding a sjambok
hippo hide
against a groom kicking a lactating bitch.
Amidst clouds of dust, the horse reared
hooves flailed, nostrils flared
while the whip slashed down on naked flesh.
Yelps and whinnies
odours of fear, sweat and urine
along with the one hurled imprecation,
"*Voetsack, skellum!*"[6]
etched themselves into Morgan's psyche.
Most memorable
when over
were Margaret's calm words called to the offender
as he hobbled away,
"*Iwe!*[7] Go to the clinic. I'll be there to treat you."
She hadn't lost her temper, had remained in control, had been teaching a
lesson.

---

[6] Get out of here!
[7] Man!

Blair's Return

In 1945
Blair returned home a hero.
The first time,
Morgan at four, saw his father
big broad intimidating
standing in the door, blocking the light,
Morgan wanted to run
hide
but resisted.
He took two tentative steps forward
then stopped
as Blair strode right past him
to shake hands with Chaka, houseboys, cook
and each of the house staff in turn.
By the time Margaret said,
"Blair, don't forget Morgan,"
Morgan had retreated
to cling to Nanny Lovely's chunky black legs.
Disgusted
Blair turned away saying,
"What's wrong with the child? Is our son a sissy?"
For Morgan the taunt became a festering sore
though later
Blair, with no experience of children,
made a vague attempt
to placate the lad
giving him a functioning watch
found in the desert from World War One.
Morgan treasured the object
yet none could have guessed
from the sullen mien worn
without fail in his father's presence.

Nanny Lovely Speaks

A Flamboyant blazed in yellow and orange
against the mid-morning blue of a Gomboli sky.
Nanny's huge and comely bulk
occupied a sturdy bench
where she crocheted yet another square
for Margaret's mile-long dining room table.
The smooth caress of yarn
silk
slid swiftly through her deft black fingers
every move defined
against a brilliant starched white pinny.
Her mind
neither on work nor surroundings
dwelt on Och-Poor-Wee-White and his parents.
She clicked her tongue
shook her head
proportioned as if carved by a sculptor.

White people!
No idea how to parent,
clever, busy, achieving,
cars, machines
gadgetry
yet no common sense
no insight into Och-Poor-Wee-White
yearning for love and attention.
Nanny Lovely put him to bed at night
helped with his prayers
liked doing it
but wasn't the job theirs?
Why did the inkos[8] not play with him?
Why the inkosikas[9] not tie him to her back
feel his heart pumping?

---

[8] . . .the boss (male)
[9] the boss (female)

Would the inkos change
knowing his son slept with the watch from the desert?
Could Margaret not show interest
in his treasures:
the papery thinness of a snake's shed skin
or the desiccated corpse of a fallen nestling?
Why didn't they show love?
Perhaps Nanny Scotlands had raised them
seemed the British way.
Nanny hauled herself to her feet and stored her crocheting
in a pretty reed basket made by her mother.
Time for Och-Poor-Wee-White's meal.

Blair

Blair's
theatrical look of younger years
had hardened
still attractive
yet drinking a bottle a day
Scotch
chain-smoking and taking no interest in Gomboli.
He never spoke of war
yet Margaret knew
its horrors rampaged through inner corridor.
She'd stroke his brow
soothe, even sing
when he woke at night shouting orders to his men.
Initially he pretended normalcy
for guests Margaret used as distraction
but soon he avoided all visitors
only once galloping out across the plains on Bucephalus
returning to the stables face stiff with rage,
"Where are the herds?" he demanded of Gwaci, a groom,
"the zebra, eland and kudu? I saw only baboon and hippo."
"The game has gone, Inkos," said Gwaci,
"too many guns, farms and fences."
Thereafter
Blair spent his days in darkened study.
Margaret and Chaka saw to his needs
no others permitted.

Nanny Lovely Speaks

Nanny Lovely settled beneath a msasa
above her head
filigree branches trapping blue speckles of sky
stitched with the blossoms of bougainvillaea.
This respite before lunch,
Nanny's favourite in the structured routines
of her working day
gave her time alone, time for thinking.
Yet today she'd barely started,
either sewing or thinking,
before Mahatchi, gardener,
drifted past
naked torso, tattered shorts and hat with a hole
greeted deferentially
African fashion
bowing his head, clapping his hands
gently.
"Good morning, Mother Mary."
Mary, name given at mission school,
liked, kept.
"What your work today, Mother?"
Nanny finished threading her needle
pointed to open box
explained,

"Name tags.
Och-Poor-Wee-Mite needs them on clothing.
He's going to boarding school."
"Always wanted to know," said Mahachi,
"Why that name for the brat?"
"I once heard Nanny Scotland say it
liked the sound
have used it ever since."
"What the meaning?"
"Don't know."
Mahatchi erupted into laughter

Nanny joining him, hilarity engulfing her whole body
while the inimitable sound of African laughter
filtered into the veld
regenerating all who heard.

Nanny dried the tears
said,
"Mahatchi, why your dislike for Och-Poor-Wee-Mite?
He's a lovely child."
"He's white. Belongs to them."
"No different to us. Laughs, plays, feeds, sleeps, pees."
"Maybe now, still young, but wait
you'll see the viper as he grows."
"He's drunk my milk. Will always be my baby."

Blair

By 1950 Blair
partially deranged
took permanently to bed
Margaret spending her days as before
but dedicating evenings to her husband.
One night dining with Blair
he in bed with a tray, she at a nearby table
realisation hit her.
At thirty seven
hair gone, skin hanging,
eyes in shadow
her heroic husband had become a wizened old man.
The green eyes flooded,
she who never cried
understood Blair was dying.
Britain's war had claimed him after all.
Facing the truth
meant giving him more time:
lunch, usually shared with Morgan,
as well as supper.

Morgan

The first time Morgan
now nine
found himself
sitting in solitary splendour
at the mile-long dining table
Nanny Lovely in attendance
resentment roiled.
Waiting till Margaret emerged from Blair's room
he confronted her,
"Mama, why didn't you lunch with me?"
"Your father's dying, Needs me. You're not dying."
Leaving, she flung a suggestion over her shoulder,
"You and Norbert take the bikes
you'll like the new tractors on Gwaai."
Morgan cheered
he'd get a driver to let him do some driving.
Mama need never know.

Funeral

Blair succumbed in 1951
Chakawia, ministering a final sip,
dispatched piccinnins for Margaret
who arrived as he died.
Morgan
away at boarding school
came home for the funeral.
saw Blair laid to rest
at the river-hut
place that looked out over land once loved.
That night alone in bed
Morgan
who since meeting his father
tried never to cry
held the desert watch to his chest
—he'd never allowed it to stop—
sobbed silently into his pillow
didn't know why
wouldn't miss the person more important to his mother
than her son.

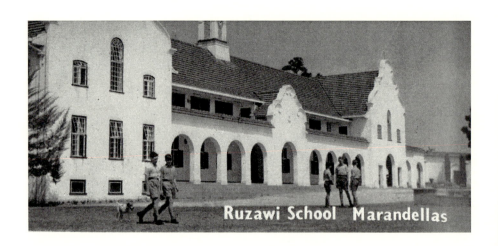

Friends

Next morning
Morgan's high spirits returned
discovering
his mother intended he stay home
for what remained of term.
He needn't go back to Ruzawi[10]
could revert to the life he loved
roaming Gomboli with his friends
chiefly Norbert, son of Nanny Lovely,
he with the same huge smile,
but also Norbert's retinue
Mweru, Mtembi, Ruka, Andrew, Sixpence
Kafumi, Keiki, Chipoko, Chifamba
Victor, Mazweeti and Marondera.
Norbert's brother Isaac
who unwittingly shared his mother's milk with Morgan,
sometimes joined the happy throng
but mostly
apprenticed to a sculptor
lived by a quarry
serpentine
not far from Umtali.

---

[10] Junior boarding school Morgan attended

With his friends, Morgan swam, fished, biked, trapped
hunted too
not only with stone and slingshot
but with a calibre .22
when able to 'borrow' a key to the gun room.

Norbert, older than Morgan,
paid by Margaret as minder
didn't do much minding.
He, his friends and Morgan
formed a ragtag band of boys roaming the land
not under Norbert but Morgan
inevitable
as lone white
referred to as Master since birth
born to lead, dominate, command.
Not merely white skin, but size, dress, bearing
reinforced the message.
Morgan chose what games to play
destinations for bikes and horses.

He rode best, shot best, won at tennis
but most important
albeit without appreciation
received a good education
first at Ruzawi, then Peterhouse.
Educational options for Norbert and company
amounted to no more than basics
plus training in a trade
as offered at the school on Gomboli.
For them non-school skills also counted
songs, dances, rhythms
ululation
knowledge of nature
tracking animal, reading weather.

At the time none cared
all were young, filled with fun,
accepting the status quo
not questioning disparity.

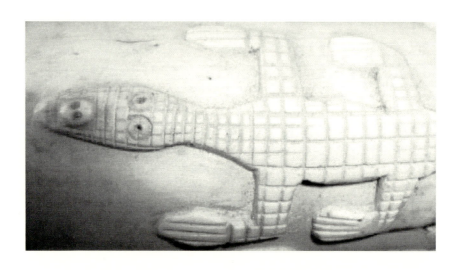

Feast on the Rocks

School holidays 1957
Morgan now sixteen
spent the morning with Norbert and friends
looking for eggs
crocodile eggs
on the banks of the Macheke, Gomboli's main river.
After long and futile search
Morgan glanced at his watch
used some choice words in Shona.
"I've missed lunch!" he explained,
"Mama won't like it."
Presence at meals was obligatory.
Norbert tut-tutted, looked sheepish
as minder might he be blamed?
"We need *skoff*[1]," said Morgan
becoming a sergeant major
firing off orders,
"You, Norbert, collect fire-wood
Mtembi, ant-eggs
Marondera, that root—yellow—I forget the name
Victor, locust

---
[1] Food

I'll raid the river hut for cooking pot, salt, mealie meal
maybe even biltong[12]
Mazweeti, come with me
you others help where needed."
It took time
but preparations complete
they crouched around the communal pot
forming with fingers
sadza balls dipped in a sauce of ant egg and tuber
gobbled
with much licking of thumb and zestful slurp.
Pièce de résistance
grilled locust
served on a sheet of tin
piccaninns used for sliding down rock.

---

[12] Dried game meat, jerkin

Margaret arrives

Thus Margaret
happened upon this rag-tag band of boys
feasting amongst granite boulder.
She'd climbed the kopjie with her three Great Danes
now off chasing a hare.
She'd intended visiting the grave
Blair's on his forty-fourth birthday
instead a scene from ancient Africa
tribesmen sharing a meal
greeted her.
On second take her eyes widened:
ancient Africa, except for one jarring anomaly
her son's white skin.
Sudden silence from his friends
alerted Morgan to her presence
he turned
froze
a dripping ball of sadza halfway to his lips.
"Knew you wouldn't go hungry," was Margaret's snide comment
Morgan liked his food.
That moment the Danes
slobbering, panting, barking joyous greeting
burst onto the scene
their tails wagging furiously
caught the boys in the face
knocking them off balance
—they crouched—
landing them in tangles of flailing arm and leg
while the pot overturned
spattering the area with hot sadza and live spark.
Margaret's vexation changed to rollicking laughter
rare since Blair departed.
Soon the boys laughed too
maybe with a little less enthusiasm
while the dogs enjoyed the remains of the food.

Confrontation

That evening in Morgan's room
as Nanny treated burns on face, arm and leg
result of flying food and ember
Umfuli, houseboy
knocked, entered, summoned Morgan to Blair's study.
Erect
sitting at magisterial desk
Margaret bade him sit.
Mistrustful he glowered at his mother
dangerous fireball
from under lowered lid.
Now forty three, eyes still vivid green
neck and figure slender
she began her lecture,
"After today's events
I've put more thought into your future."
Ominous!
"But, Mama, it's decided
after A-levels, Rhodes."
"I've changed my mind. England."
"No, Mama!"
Unwittingly he kicked Suki
Great Dane
under the table
felt her yelp was his.
"I won't leave Africa!"
Margaret remained unfazed.
"You have no option. I've made up my mind."

He squirmed.
"Why the change?"
"I'd overlooked the fact you're going native.
Certain attributes
nicety in manner, dress and speech
are second nature to the English gentleman.
We, your family, require you comply
it's your duty
price you pay for the blood that runs in your veins."
Morgan spluttered in rage as she continued,
"Four years at an English university will do the trick."
"This is home!" he blurted. "I'm African not English.
I don't **want** to be an English gentleman.
I didn't **ask** for the blood that runs in my veins!"
"Don't argue, Morgan. It's not for you to ask
it's for me to ordain.
Get changed.
You look ridiculous. Like a leopard."
"They're burns!"
"I'm aware of their provenance."
He detected a repressed smile
with sudden insight understanding
she'd been playing with him
mocking him.
As he turned to leave, Suki following
Margaret added,
"I expect to see you for dinner in twenty minutes."
Nodding he left
placing as he went
a hand on the dog's silken head.
If Suki, the bitch, could forgive
what did that make his unforgiving mother?

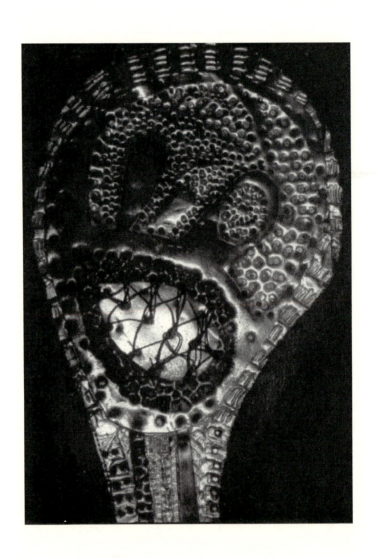

Nanny Lovely and Morgan

As Nanny dabbed delicately at a blister
Morgan said, "At home you'll need to do the same for Norbert."
"The boys will go to the clinic
The mutti[13] there's the same as here."
"True. They'll recover. I won't".
"What do you mean, Och?" Anxious, Nanny moved round to peer into his face.
"I told you. Mama's exiling me to England."
She tut-tutted, clicked her tongue.
"Don't talk like that. I'll miss you, but it's opportunity. Education."
He swore in Shona.
Hand to her mouth, eyes big
torn between shock and laughter, Nanny asked,
"Who taught you that, Och?"
"Norbert."

---

[13] Medicine

Laughter took the upper hand and they laughed together,
Morgan's guffaw providing the bass to Nanny's more musical soprano.
As Nanny packed up salve and unction, she resumed her lecture.
"You should appreciate education. Norbert doesn't have these
opportunities."
"Norbert can go instead," said Morgan. "I'll swop.
Can you imagine what Mama would say?"
Both laughed again uproariously
Nanny clapping her hands and slapping her knees
Morgan drumming on the table.

Morgan in England

Morgan dragged out A-levels as long possible
but finally met the requirements.
September second, 1959
Margaret drove him
silent and sullen
to Salisbury airport.
Why wouldn't she let him drive?
No doubt another non-too-subtle message.
At the airport
he declined a snack
unheard of
refused to show interest in an unusual aircraft
and checked into departures too early.
Striding to the plane
he didn't look back
—was she still there?—
nor lifted his eyes from his book
till out of Rhodesia
dinner pending.

Carolyn

Morgan
having determined in advance
he'd detest England, family and university
the attitude proved self-fulfilling
until help arrived in the form of Carolyn
who struck up conversation one night
leaving the library.
As they angled across the quad
she commented,
"You study harder than anyone I know
you're always here till closing."
"I want to finish, get back home."
"You don't like England?
"Well . . ."
He hummed, hah-ed, attempting politeness
then suddenly
finding himself with gorgeous girl
big-boned, slender, sleek black hair
heard himself enthuse,
"I love the architecture."
Together they looked up at mystic gothic spire.
"I also love the cars, trees
history, fish and sea.
I suppose my relations aren't that bad either."

One winter evening
Carolyn and her friend Martha
took a brief break from their studies.
"You've made quite a catch," said Martha
munching a cookie.
"Meaning?"
"Morgan, of course. Who else? Stereotype alpha male."
Disliking the conversation
Carolyn blew on her tea
remembered her nanny saying, "Don't do that, child. It's vulgar."
"Well isn't he?" Martha persisted
"Isn't he what?"
"Alpha male."
"If you say so."
"I do. I also say you could do worse
nice blonde hair, straight nose, well-muscled, big,
perhaps though . . ."

"What?"
"A bit of a rough diamond."
Carolyn sprang to defend,
"Poor dear is caught between two worlds
doesn't come from here
he's colonial
theatres and concerts
dances
shop, museum, pub, gallery
haven't featured in his world
but all is easily cured.
He's from good family, is already changing.
Let's get back to work."
From the inward smile on Martha's face
Carolyn recognized
she'd revealed more than intended.

Return to Gomboli

For Morgan
time now passed more pleasantly
more rapidly
yet still he hankered for home
so
as soon as both graduated, he married Carolyn
in the traditional manner required by the families
whisked her back to Gomboli.

As the car drew up
in front of the house on the kopjie
Morgan felt like removing shoe and sock
doing a war-dance
as always with Norbert and gang
on his return from school.
Clapping, ululating, singing
they always followed the car
vying to open the door
shake his hand.
Now there was nothing
no Norbert, no gang, no hoopla.
Hiding disappointment
he took Carolyn by the arm
shepherding her to the front door of Gomboli
all the while listening
hoping to hear the boys arriving.
He heard nothing
only the 'go-away' bird.

Entrance

Margaret studied the young woman in the doorway
as she adjusted to the hall
where clusters of white clad servants
waited to greet her.
Margaret liked what she saw
a sensible nice looking upper class girl.
She gave her daughter-in-law time to adapt
then stepped forward
arms spread saying,
"Carolyn, my dear, welcome!"
From the corner of her eye she noted Morgan's surprise
she rarely greeted with such effusion.
He'd soon see other changes
even Nanny Lovely wasn't there to meet him.

Talk with Chaka

With Carolyn resting in their room
Morgan tiptoed out
ordered a servant to tell Chakawia
Blair's loyal servant
to meet him at the pool away from prying eye.
Sitting on low veranda wall
Morgan questioned Chaka
standing before him in robe and fez.
"Tell me, my friend,
where are Norbert, Mweru. Mtembi, Ruka, Andrew, Sixpence and the rest?"
Chaka lowered his eyes, wrung his hands
didn't speak.
"Answer me, Chaka . . . I must know."
"They've gone, Inkos!"
Inkos! Only Blair had been Inkos
at stake though were bigger matters.
"Gone! Gone where?"
"Away, Inkos."
"Not good enough, Chaka."
"To the bush."
It felt like pulling porcupine quills
from the head of a nosey dog
but slowly the information came.
"Trouble's ahead, Inkos
young men restless, want the land, all of it."
The land!
Morgan hid the shock that left him short of breath
while Chaka
eyes to the ground
fought his own emotions.
"How will they get the land?"
Morgan feared he knew the answer
Chaka confirmed it,

"You hand over the farm, Inkos, or they'll take it."
"With the gun?"
"How else?"
"That makes them terrorists."
"They have another name. Freedom fighters."
"Terror's easy to learn
not so governing
not so using the land to feed others."
Chaka shook his head
"I don't know, Inkos. I fear for us all.
They bring in arms."
"From where?"
"Russia. Stash them around the country
mostly in outlying area."
"Norbert too?"
Chaka nodded, didn't speak
couldn't speak
unshed tears gleamed in rheumy eyes.
Morgan,
in an unusual gesture of affection,
placed a big hand on the other's back.
"Thank you for talking, Chaka.
One more thing
where's Nanny Lovely?"
"Busy keeping the peace.
You'll see her tomorrow
prepare for change
she no longer laughs or sings
barely speaks
either here or in the compound."
Morgan turned away saying,
"Poor Nanny. Loves everyone. Never could takes sides."
He felt as though he'd swallowed a bottle of bleach.

Dinner

Morgan barely got though the motions
of changing into dinner jacket for Margaret's welcoming dinner.
He'd be sitting at Jacobean table
dining on salmon from Scotland
while Norbert, Mweru,
Mtembi, Maswiti, Katiki, Machya, Manara, Samuel, Umbati, Andrew,
Kafumi, Kieki, Umfuli
guerilla fighters, outlaws, bandits one and all
skulked around the bush
eating sadza and termite
plotting the demise for every white in Rhodesia.

"You're unusually quiet," said Margaret
preparing to sample a dollop of soufflé.
"We've had a long journey, Mama."
"That might be
but my conversation with your beautiful wife
might have interested you."
Morgan looked at his mother wide-eyed.
Beautiful wife!
It wasn't a Margaret-like comment
but looking at Carolyn
determined she did indeed look lovely
dress from Dior
hair
long, sleek, black and shiny.
"I mentioned to Carolyn," said Margaret,
"I've bought a house in Salisbury.
Gomboli is now yours."

Night Visit to the River Hut

With Carolyn asleep in exhaustion
Morgan again slipped away
this time to the stables
finding comfort in the horses
their smell, their bulk, their stamping, their snorting.
What contrast to nights in Oxford and London!
On looking through the tack-room
he succumbed to a sudden impulse
saddled Bruce
progeny of Blair's Bucephalus and galloped off
across the moonlit veld
to the river-hut.

Up on the rock
wandering among giant boulder
looking out over the moonlit land
his land
he tried to still the myriad images
tumbling about in his head:
buried weaponry
mine, grenade, bandolier, AK
intermingled with vivid mental pictures
huts burning
black families trapped inside
on purpose
white farmers gunned down in their own front doorways.

Standing on a rock near Blair's grave
Morgan found himself conducting
in his mind
an internal dialogue with Norbert.
He pictured his erstwhile friend
sullen and belligerent on a nearby rock.
"Can't we compromise?" he asked.
"No," snapped Norbert," no compromises!
We'll take what we want, whether you like it or not."
"What is it you want?"
"The land. All of it. It's ours."
"You wouldn't use it productively
you don't have the skills."
"You didn't teach us."
"You are many, we are few, one to your twenty."
"True, but what happens to the land isn't important
if it returns to bush, so be it
it's ours, not yours, you stole it."

"My parents bought it
legally."
"You made the laws. Ours are different."
"I don't want to fight, Norbert."
"Then hand over the land."
"No."
"Then we fight."
"We were friends, Norbert. I hope we still are."
"Friends not equals. Without land there's no parity."
"I find it abhorrent, but if I have to I'll fight."
"No matter how long it takes, Morgan,
you never can win."
Heeding the summons of his restless horse
Morgan suppressed the imaginary polemic
headed back to the house on the kopjie.

Nanny Lovely and Morgan

Before dawn the next morning
Morgan found Nanny in the kitchen.
"Nanny, we'll have tea together in my room
my old one.
Jeremiah will make it."
Face serious, she settled in her accustomed seat
big old chair by the window.
He, hands between knees, sat perched on a stool at her side.
"Tell me, Nanny, about Norbert and Isaac."
"Isaac's fine.
He has sculptures at the Rhodes National Gallery."
"Fantastic! I look forward to seeing them."
"The inkosikas bought one. Big!"
She pointed upward. "Higher than the ceiling.
Stone. In the garden by the fountain."
"You'll show me as soon it's light."
She beamed with pride.
"Norbert? How's he?"
Nanny's face turned heavy
she moved to the edge of the chair,
"In old times, Och, our young men had status, dignity, function
now no longer, they want land, want to govern."
'What do you think, Nanny?'
"I understand their need, but don't want violence
don't want guns."

"Nor I."
"For me, Och, education matters more than land."
"No, Nanny. Norbert's right. It's land."
Nanny sighed, inclined her head
a fat tear coursed down rounded cheek.
Morgan tried for levity,
"Sorry, Nanny, we leopards don't change our spots."
"Couldn't you try, Och, you and Norbert?"
"Norbert's my friend, always will be, but . . ."
They sat in silence, then Morgan poured tea, gave Nanny a cup.
Usually she poured, she served.
They sipped in silence then Nanny said,
"You have a lovely wife, Och,"
She hadn't yet met Carolyn but perhaps had heard.
"Are you happy?"
"Would be if I didn't fear for the future. Wonder if she'll cope.
Doesn't love Africa like we do."
"She must love you."
"I hope so, but will it be enough?"
Light from the rising sun caught the remnants of Nanny's tears.
"Come, Nanny," said Morgan. "We'll go and see Isaac's sculpture."
He helped her out of the chair and together they left the house
arm in arm, through the front door.

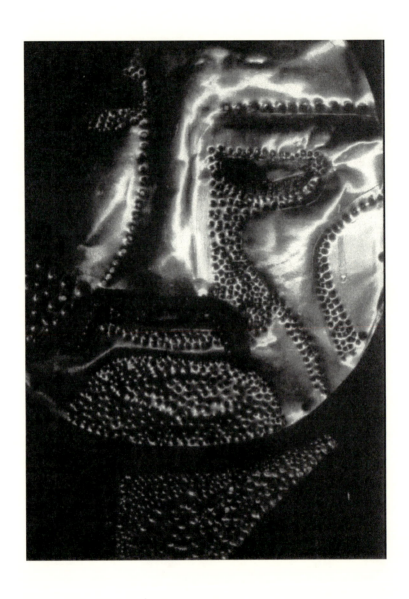

Civil War

Civil war broke out officially in 1965
when governing whites under Ian Smith
wanting to maintain standards
declared unilateral independence from Britain.
Bad day for Margaret and Carolyn
this split from native land
yet what option
in the face of Britain's duplicity
insisting on black majority rule
knowing full well
this exposed kith and kin
to ignorance and savagery.
Shameless ingratitude
to those who fought Britain's war!
Blair was one
there were many more.

Initially remoter regions
suffered most from the insurgents
then terror spread to the core.
By 1975 in spite of white denial
none could pretend
strikes on bridge, road, pylon, dam
didn't happen.
Attacks too on white farms grew
moving closer to the capital.
As white civilians fled, as white troops fell
—body bags without number—
fewer remained to fight the growing ranks of black soldiery.
Soon all white males
regardless of job, age, status
received call-up papers
amongst them Morgan
till then considered more useful on Gomboli.

Margaret Returns to Gomboli

Without Morgan
Carolyn now with two young sons
couldn't remain alone in the house on the kopjie
so she and Margaret swopped
Carolyn moving to Salisbury
Margaret dusting off boot and jodhpur
returning to Gomboli.
Arriving she knew right away
things had changed
she'd stepped into a world
for which even she intrepid woman
was ill-equipped.
The stone-walled house was now a fort
doors barred with steel, sandbags in the windows.
Twice single-handedly
Morgan had fought off multiple insurgents
with rocket, grenade, machine gun and mortar.
Outdoors
Margaret learnt of ham strung cattle
slashed crops
animals battered to pulp with gun butts.
She received news of neighbouring farmers
of loyal servants
slaughtered, maimed, burned or blown apart.

She herself noticed amongst the Africans
a change in mood.
Wary, sullen, fearful,
they no longer laughed or sang
condition exacerbated
by foreign white mercenaries in Gomboli's new militia
a menacing presence
always in evidence
guarding buildings, installations, protecting workers and transport
from ambush, landmine, sabotage
all mammoth tasks without the most important:
keeping insurgents out of the compounds.
Margaret knew the task was impossible
too big for militia or army.
Whites were losing the war
yet government not wishing to hurry the end
disguised the truth
saying if everyone played their part
whites still could win.

Children

One afternoon
with jacarandas in full and glorious bloom
Margaret protected by a guard
inspected discarded metal
near the barns.
The dogs snuffling about seeking errant rodent
suddenly froze, pricked their ears
set up furious barking.
Before they could attack
Margaret called them back, shouting to the guard,
"Don't shoot!"
She recognised the man who ran to meet her
a teacher
breathing ragged
face bathed in sweat.
"Inkosikas," he wailed, "the children have gone."
"Gone! Gone where?"
"The men of the night took them, entered the school with guns
herded them together
marched them into the bush."
"What for?"
"To train, Inkosikas."
"They're children!"
"The bigger ones they use in combat
the others as mujibas."
"Mujibas?"
"Messengers."
"The militia must follow!"
"No, Inkosikas!
If you use the militia they'll kill the children."

A difficult Night

That night
Margaret's bed was a mattress
shared with dogs
on the bathroom floor.
She spent each night in a different space
bathroom, bunker, pantry being safest
least accessible to rocket, bullet, mortar and grenade.
Trying to make space for herself between hulking canines
she felt old, leached, desiccated
not because of loneliness
not because of fear
because
except for Blair's death,
she'd never faced a problem she couldn't solve.

Now
although badly in need of sleep
multiples worries left her no peace.
How expect loyalty from employees
when loyalty brought serious consequence?
Conversely
how mistrust blacks she'd known for over thirty years?
Knew their children, their grandchildren
saw them as extended family.
Insufferable!
She tossed
all the while conscious of her weaponry
rocket in the corner, grenade under the pillow
rifle by the tub.
Despite appropriate training
she wondered if she could ever use them.

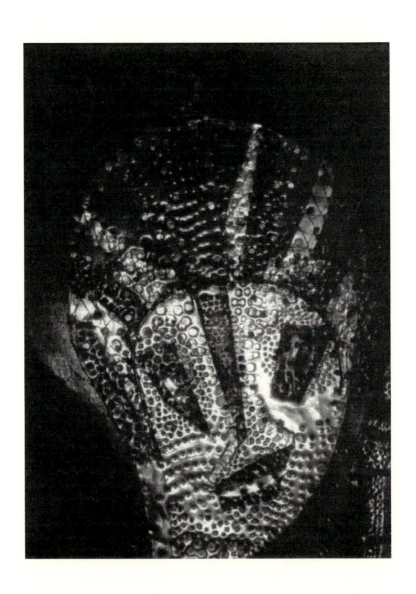

Margaret meets her Nemesis

Around 1 p.m. she fell asleep
only to awaken to the ferocious barking of dogs.
She got up
put on slippers and dressing gown
—white silk from Spain—
rifle in hand, went to the front door.
The three dogs
hackles bristling
mouths distorted in vicious snarls
pranced
ready for attack.
Someone outside pleaded,
"Inkosikas, Inkosikas, it's Chakawia. Open please."
Over the noise of the dogs and the thud of her own heart
Margaret couldn't tell if the voice was really Chaka's.
Through the years
similar situations had arisen
she'd always responded.
Now it might be a set-up
or might be true
If Chaka needed help, she wouldn't want to fail him.
Never lacking in courage
—spitfire had been a childhood name—
she set aside her rifle, used both hands to lift the bar
unbolted the door
opened it.
A spotlight blazed in her face
blinded her.
She saw nothing.

What those outside saw
frozen in the beam
standing proud in the doorway of Gomboli
a slender woman in flowing robe
long neck, halo of black hair
one hand gripped a dog by the collar
dog the size of a pony
the other shaded her eyes.
The image lasted a second
then shattered
in a salvo of shrieking bullet.

Moments later
the door of Gomboli hung on its hinges
snagged on splinters of teak:
dog fur, silk and a clump of black hair
lodged in a speck of white scalp.

From granite flagstone
insurgent leader Mweru appropriated as momento
an undamaged slipper
which he stored with care in a pocket.
No time for pillage
the militia alerted by the shooting
was en route
headlights lurching up the road
to the house on the kopjie.

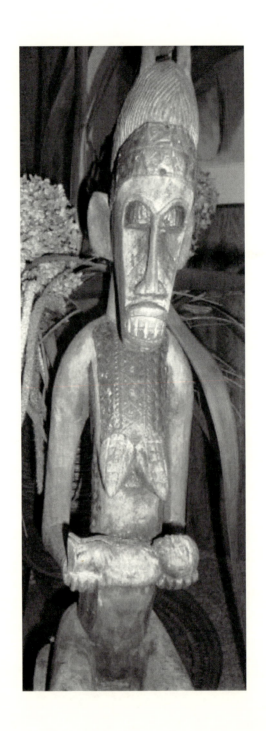

Nanny Lovely

In spite of curfew, in spite of danger
Nanny ran barefoot
taking the short-cut up to house
arriving before the militia.
With a howl
she threw herself at Margaret's mutilated body
settling on the flagstones
gathering it into her arms, cradling it like a child
keening
eee . . . eee . . . eee . . . eeeeeeeee.

Morgan returns to Gomboli

Released by the military
Morgan returned to Gomboli.
carrying within him
lead
that blocked all thought, emotion, feeling
allowing him to focus
only on the job.
Thus he'd functioned in the forces
so again now
organizing Margaret's funeral
repairing the door
constructing a second grave at the river hut.
The only chore that afforded the slightest pleasure:
purchase of three Great Dane pups
their antics helping him ban the horror
continue as he knew he must.

He phoned Carolyn and the children on a regular basis
with Nanny's help
remembering birthday, anniversary, Christmas
also visiting
but never allowing their visits
not even for Margaret's funeral.
He used danger as the excuse
valid
yet he also knew that his family
had the right to expect more of him than he could give.
Having difficulty placing one foot in front of the other
he finally understood what war had done to his father.

Message

At lunchtime on September 19th, 1977
Morgan was opening mail
when Nanny Lovely knocked on the door
bringing lunch on a tray
as requested.
He cleared a space, thanked her
returned to the bills.
Nanny remained at the desk
unusual
hands clasped over her stomach
head bent
eyes cast down like a pious saint.
She had something to say, waited for attention.
He raised his eyes,
"What is it, Nanny?"
She rushed her reply, "Norbert sends a message."
"Norbert!"

They no longer spoke of Norbert
yet Morgan found him
again and again
lingering in the corners of his mind.
"Norbert says if you can trust him
he too will trust.
He'll meet you this evening
at dusk
at the river-hut."
Morgan blanched beneath his tan
a pulse thudded in his eardrum
yet his voice remained steady,
"I'm listening, Nanny. Proceed."
"You must go alone. No militia. He too will come unaccompanied.
You may bring your rifle
he'll bring his but won't shoot first."

Meeting

As Morgan parked his armoured vehicle
at the foot of the kopjie.
every cell tingled in electric awareness.
This could be a set-up
yet he'd kept his part of the bargain
the militia
unaware of the meeting
ate in their barracks before nightly patrol.
Rifle ready
he climbed the path
to the boulder-strewn plateau.
His senses focussed, he looked, listened, sniffed
found no telltale signs of trap
no footprints
no broken grass, cigarette butts or wrapper
nothing.
Reaching the top he wandered amongst towering boulder
settling on a rock near his parents' graves
FN across his knees
he waited.
Below
dusk closed in across the land.
Whose land? His? Theirs?

Norbert came from behind, calling
"Morgan!"
The tone held unmistakable warmth.
Morgan stood, turned
slowly
rifle directed to the ground.
He saw before him a powerful man
heavy boot and camo
in one hand an AK
the other stretched in greeting.
In the half-light
Morgan recognized nothing of this person
except the ready smile
Nanny Lovely's
familiar since earliest childhood.
It was enough
in spite of himself he felt a frisson of pleasure
couldn't help it
he too smiled, took the proffered hand.

Together they walked amongst the boulders
"Your mother . . .," Norbert began
Morgan helped him, "Were you there?"
"No. Was away. Heard later."
"Heard what?"
"That she opened the door."
"I assumed so. She was alone and the bar out of place."
"Why? She knew the dangers."
"I don't know."
"She'd have been OK otherwise."
"Maybe she was tired like I am. That's why I'm here."
Norbert, extracted a couple of cigarettes
gave one to Morgan, lit them, continued,
"Both you and I have killed yet unlike some
we're not born killers.
All I want is land. Not killing."
"Ah, the land," sighed Morgan.
Together they looked out over the veld
bathed in light of a rising moon.
Without speaking they turned back to the graves
Morgan finally saying,
"Tell me, Norbert, where's Chakawia?"
"Dead. Same night as your mother. He was loyal. Refused to betray."
"Maybe Chaka too was tired."
"I think so."
"I've been wanting this meeting," said Morgan,
"but you arranged it. Why?
Do you believe there's a thread that binds us
you and me, black and white?"

Finis

Norbert had no chance to reply
as a fury of bullet
crack of AK
ricocheted around the boulders and out over the land.
Morgan tried to lift his rifle
but it fell from his hands as Norbert
hit by a barrage of bullets
careened into him with the force of a truck.
Then Morgan too was lifted and spun
as fire from barking automatics
slammed into every part of his anatomy.
Amidst exploding pain
one last thought took shape
they had kept the faith
he and Norbert
a thread existed.

Magazines empty
—thirty shots from each of nine guns—
firing stopped.
Mweru led his men from behind the rocks
checking corpses:
broken
tangled
limbs at odd angles
glazed in a sheen of blood.
Together Mweru, Kafumi and Ruka
separated the bodies
tossing Morgan onto his mother's grave
where he landed
disjointed, crumpled
head over the edge.
They straightened Norbert as best they could.
"Pity," said Mweru. "A good man
but too close to the other
together
too infrangible, too cohesive, too strong."
Taking guns and ammo
the men dissolved into shadow.

Nanny Lovely

Panting
Nanny struggled up the kopjie
to be met by the sight of her child
laid out in moonlight.
She threw herself at him
trying to gather him into her arms
not managing, changing tactic.
Settling with her back to a rock
legs straight ahead
she pulled Norbert across her lap
all the while keening.
Suddenly she stopped
turned
saw Morgan slumped across his mother's grave.
In agonized howl shouted, "Isaac!"
knew he'd followed
was hiding.
Emerging Isaac begged in hoarse whisper,
"Come, Mama! We must go. Please!"
"No! Bring me my Och!"

He obeyed
laying Morgan over his mother's lap alongside Norbert.
With huge arms across both, Nanny closed her eyes
alternating the high-pitched notes of ancient lament
with keening that penetrated
every hut, den and burrow on the veld
eee . . . eee . . . eeeeeeee.

"Come, Mama!" Isaac pleaded, "The militia . . ."
She lifted her head, "I'll stay, son.
It's you that must go."
As Isaac faded from view
Nanny Lovely closed her eyes and rocking back and forth
sang quietly
entering a trance-like state.

Militia

Amidst the crackle of radio, bristling rifles and stomping boot
the militia arrived led by a hard-bitten Kiwi.
"Jesus!" he swore
trying to make sense of the scene:
Nanny Lovely sitting amongst towering boulder
face serene
lifted to the moon
singing a melody never before heard.
He shivered
suddenly realizing that in the shadows across her lap
lay two bodies.
"A pietà," he whispered,
"a bloody African pietà!"
Then addressing his men,
"The bastards got them both."
"Is she round the bend?" asked one of Nanny Lovely.
"Nah. She's just a mother
an African mother."

Epilogue

Carolyn London sophisticate
widow to Morgan, mother of two
initially followed events in Africa
knew that in 1980
Rhodesia became Zimbabwe
blacks governing under Robert Mugabe.
Carolyn remained informed
till told
Mugabe had gifted Gomboli
still legally hers
to his wife as a birthday bauble.
Thence forwards
Carolyn
wishing to spare her nerves
avoided news from Africa
till one day she received by mail
an envelope
with a big splashy stamp of a stalking leopard
inside an invitation to a gallery in London

Shed Snake Skins
Sculptures by Isaac Masenda
Opening reception 2-4 pm.
She attended with her sons and found welcome in a huge smile
Nanny Lovely's
beaming from the face of Isaac.

Eventually she bought the gallery
specialized in African art
sent the proceeds to Mother Mary's Orphanage
although Nanny Lovely herself had long since retired.

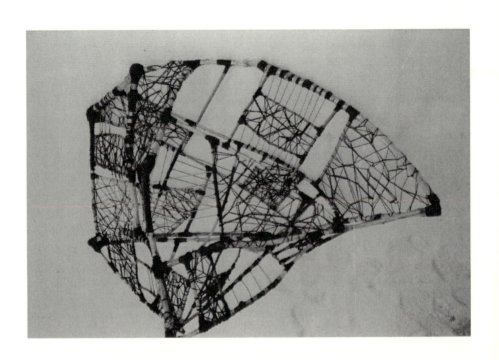

Haitian Girl

In early August, 1980
Hurricane Allen
Category 5
struck Haiti.
Lucille's father was outside
attempting repair
when a high wind
strafed the ground sending roofing
tin
through the air to decapitate paterfamilias.
In addition
when Allen moved on
goat, home and coffee crop too
had gone
leaving Mamma Michelle, Lucille and her younger siblings
standing in mud
knee-high
with nothing.
Mamma Michelle knew without doubt that the spirits
loa
displeased for transgression unknown
had meted out punishment.
Appeasement was needed.
If Hurricane Allen had not taken

Iemenja, Papa Baron and Chango
statuettes of her favourite voodoo deities
she would have placed at their feet and felt better
offerings of hibiscus and mango
but now she must travel long distance on foot
to rituals
where song, dance and drum
lifted the screen to reveal
the world of the spirit.
By attending such ceremony
Mamma Michele left behind her offspring
to salvage what they could from debris and mud.
The eldest,
five-year old Lucille
out of her depth
in shock, confused
attached herself when possible
to a missionary couple from Canada.
The husband
Lucille called him Mister but might have said Papa
was an architect by profession but had set aside his job
in favour of religious vocation.
Lucille hung on every word he uttered
thus one day hearing him mention
that the long saga of Haitian disaster
would be half as bad
if someone had bothered to create
proper habitat.
"A good architect," he said,
"could produce with ease
lightweight dwellings to protect from rain and sun
withstand extreme and capture ocean breeze."

He illustrated the idea to his interlocutor
with drawings of skeletal structures
he then scrunched and discarded.
Lucille watched
listened
grasping only half his meaning
but retrieving the crumpled paper.
Perplexed, Mister asked her reason.
"When big," she explained,
"I'll make places to keep us safe."
He studied the child
dirt-streaked cheek, malodorous, tattered
but a face alight with fervour.
Patting the matted head he told her,
"First you need to study architecture."
Yes!" She jumped up and down clapping,
"I'll study arc . . . . sher!"
Bending to her level
his speech slow and kind he said,
"Copy me, Lucille, arc . . . it . . . ec . . . tsh . . . er."
"I'll study architecture," she proclaimed
pronunciation perfect.
He didn't feel like explaining
such things didn't happen in Haiti.
Lucille used her new word
architecture
ad nauseam
irritating peer and adult alike.

Meanwhile on the island
disease ran amok
rioting a daily occurrence.
One morning early
Mamma Michele
minuscule scrap of abused humanity
sought out Mister.
She carried a child on her back, dragged another by the arm
and wore perched on her head
not her size
a salvaged wig.
Dropping to her knees she stretched out her hand
entreating,
"Please, Mister, take Lucille when you leave."
Mister tried to help her to her feet
she resisted, reasoned, pleaded,
"She's a good child, chance is all she needs."
"I know, madam.
It breaks my heart but it's not feasible.
There are millions like Lucille."
"But, sir, she's different
special.
Unlike others
she saw her papa lose his head
sight no child should ever see."
Mamma Michele had played her trump
albeit not factual:
she alone
had seen the tin roof fly and kept concealed the detail.
Mister relented.

In Canada
on her first day at kindergarten
Lucille gathered a handful of sticks
forsythia prunings left by a negligent gardener.
When asked to leave them behind
she declined
when told they were trash
tantrum
Given permission to keep them
she produced a cherubic smile.
When offered toys, only playdough pleased.
With this she joined her sticks
turning two dimensions into three.
Each day in recess she restocked with twig,
sifting, sorting, accepting, rejecting
knowing exactly what she needed.
With time
her strange skeletal structures
initially crude and inept
improved and she began filling the gaps
with paper, fabric and string.

Through the years
as brightest star
Lucille received the best in education
landing finally
in the London offices of famed female Iraqui architect
Zaha Hadid
with whom Lucille, as woman and outsider, identified.
At Hadid's she worked on such iconic projects
as the CAC[14] in Cincinnati and the MAXXI[15] in Rome
She earned well
lived well

---

[14] Contemporary Art Centre
[15] Museum of 21st Century Art

found a suitable boyfriend
in the person of Zebadiah from Zimbabwe
also an architect
white-skinned and dashing.

Lucille's stick fabrications
now masqueraded as sculptures
receiving much acclaim for imagination and beauty.
Yet Haiti remained her goal and when she heard from a friend
that Mamma Michele had broken a bone
she pulled up stakes
together with Zeb and his dog Iver
returned to the island.
There they made prototypes of homes
tailored to Haitian need.
They were dome-like
with a pedigree reaching back through the years
to Lucille's pre-school era
but using instead of sticks
prefabricated strut and high tech filling.
Soon Lucille and Zeb with Iver
occupied on the beach
two individual streamlined structures.
There they lived in comfort
refreshed by breezes and unscathed by gale or rain.

By the beginning of 2009
they were ready for full-scale production
lacking nothing but a rubber stamp
from an elusive local leader.
Month after month they waited
to no avail.
They changed tactic, became proactive
threatening to lay bare corruption
name names
go public with their frustration.
They also presented an ultimatum
deadline for Wednesday, January 13, 2010.

On that day
Lucille climbed out of bed
expecting to enjoy the sunrise over water.
Instead
she narrowly missed striking her face
on something suspended
head height in her entrance:
a crudely carved doll
vest bloodied
a nail through the chest.
Recognising the Haiti of her youth
voodoo
had returned to claim to her
she ran
mouth dry, eyes wide, breathing erratic
along the edge of the surf to Zeb's.
No one came to greet her.

Finally she found Zeb digging a hole in the palm grove
a blood-soaked mound
in a sheet at his feet.
Voice flat, he told her,
"I failed Iver.
Someone hacked him to death in the night and I heard nothing."
Tears streaked his cheek while Lucille clutched herself
trying to keep together the bits
stop her chin trembling
her teeth chattering.
Her voice cracked and broken she said,
"We have to leave, Zeb!
"Get out. Now. Today!"
He looked up from his digging
eyebrows raised in surprise,
"Abandon the domes?"
"We must! This is witchcraft."
"Do we bow to such pressure?"
Lucille's words emerged in a rush,
"You have to believe me. You weren't born in Haiti
don't understand.
There's no option. We must leave.
Now. Today."
Zeb stood silent and watching as Lucille continued,
"To the outsider spirits, witchcraft, spell, trance, curse
might seem idiotic
yet they have a life of their own
worm their way into the mind
feed from within.

The loa,
spirit world,
whatever you wish to call it
exists and cannot be ignored.
It lures me back to the fold.
We must go!"
Zeb abandoned his stance
came to hold her
trying to control her shaking.
"Don't you think, dear," he suggested,
"we give power to what we believe?
Isn't it through our credence
that this evil exists?"
"It's real, Zeb. Very real. I feel the pull. It'll triumph."
She clawed at him.
"We must go!"
"And so we shall," he soothed
gently releasing her cast iron grip.
"After what's happened to Iver
I too am uncomfortable."
He lifted the bloody bundle
holding it like a slumbering child
lowered it into the hole
which together
they filled with the red earth of Haiti.

That afternoon Lucille and Zeb
tried to convince Mamma Michele to leave with them.
"I won't go," she announced
chin stuck out, arms akimbo.
"But you must, Mamma, we want you
can't assist from afar.
Life will be good, easier
electricity, clean water, machines."
"Well . . .," began Mamma Michele, eyes dancing.
Lucille grabbed the chance,
"That's decided.
We'll help you pack
just a few essentials."
Mama Michele hobbled to her voodoo figurines
Iemanja, Chango and Papa Baron.
"I'll pack you guys first," she assured them.
Aghast Lucille protested,
"Mama we want to escape them! They belong in Haiti!"
Mamma Michele straightened
her face as fierce as vengeful deity
pointed an accusing finger
proclaimed in thunderous voice,
"You rob me my gods!"
Shocked
Lucille and Zeb
stood side by side staring.
It was 4:58
the time the earthquake struck.

Lucille
pinned under rubble, drifted in and out of lucidity
knowing that somewhere close at hand
Zeb lay dead
maybe Mamma Michele as well but she wasn't certain.
Briefly she asked herself the Haitian question
why the loa's rage?
what their need for restitution?
She waited, but feeling no resonance,
understood
with unprecedented incontrovertibility
that she'd always placed faith
in goodness and loving
allowing evil no purchase
no nurture
no muscle.
She was therefore now in goodly hand
not victim to vengeful Haitian god.
With thought and feeling
receding
Lucille wondered in passing,
if the domes had survived the quake.

The had.
Although tattered
they still stood intact on the beach as before.
In years ahead
will strangers still ask, "What are those?"
Or maybe such homes will be standard.

Actor

As every morning of his working life
Farley woke
and swung his legs to the bedside carpet.
Such fun being an actor!
Audience, applause, acclaim, camaraderie
but above all the sublimity of living in another's skin
seeing through another's eyes.
Whose eyes would it be today?
It vaguely surprised him that the pertinent persona
usually determined by one of his recent roles
had not immediately sprung to mind
a mind that had always acted with feline alacrity
probing the deepest facets of human specificity.
This was the basis for his brilliance as a consummate mimic
the reason why, even as a child, he could adopt with ease
gait, speech, manner, mien
of anyone he encountered.
Now when he should be combing his hair
as perhaps a modern day Lear
he was still cogitating,
lacking options for a suitable person for the day.
He remonstrated with himself
tried to conquer the inertia,
"Think, Farley, think!
Who should you be today?"
Might he use one of those men in . . . .

He couldn't remember the drama's title
nor playwright
nor protagonists' names.
Nothing.
Something unpleasant niggled in his head
Without warning a woollen blanket
wet, heavy
seemed to fall from the ceiling, pinning him to the bed.
He'd suddenly remembered what he'd forgotten since waking:
he'd left the stage
voluntarily and permanently
for botching his lines
only once
when his memory had failed.
Had he overreacted?
Alas, too late, the deed was done.
He dropped his head to his hands
howled
tears poured through his fingers
drenching sheet and shirt.
He couldn't stop, didn't want to
no one would hear.
He lived alone on Queen Street in an old Victorian villa
near the theatre, that lovely theatre!
The thought brought new vigour to his caterwauling
but after a while his throat hurt
he'd always protected it
voice was everything
so he tried to distract himself
focus on his home
through the years lovingly restored
now a source of inordinate pride.

Spreading his fingers
he saw sashes
skirting board
both recently enhanced with golden ash.
Surprisingly the sight brought little comfort
the sobs resumed rising to new crescendo.
He reached for the phone
dialled his friend
also recently retired but well adjusted.
"Ald," he blubbered, "I have no persona for today
can't get off the bed, feel like concrete."
Aldgate's voice, mellifluous and soothing,
flowed from the phone
"I understand, Far, I've been there
but now it pleases me to be myself
the real me."
"But, Ald," Farley blurted, "There's no real me!
I've always been someone else."
The wailing persisted
until finally Aldgate's prolonged silence registered.
Panicking Farley screamed down the line
"Are you there, Ald? Did you hear?
Answer! Don't leave me, I'll die!"
"You exaggerate, Far," replied Aldgate the tone low and kindly,
"I'm listening, waiting till you settle."
"Sorry, Ald," Farley snivelled.
Aldgate's voice became strong and authoritarian
the one he used in Henry V,
"Listen carefully, Far, follow my words to the letter."
With Aldgate in charge Farley felt better.
"Get yourself up," Aldgate ordered. "Do it. Now. Is it done?

Good! Next take the phone
go to your closet
find that shirt with the Stratford logo . . ."
Aldgate talked Farley through every move
finally getting him to the door saying,
"You're on your own now, Far.
You'll cross the park, head for the Avon.
On the way you'll focus on everything you see
and because you are
sorry, we are
getting older and our memories failing,"
renewed sobs from Farley
"you'll take notes on that pad
I told you to put in your pocket."

It was an autumn day in October
with damp tree trunks rising like Gothic pillars
through leaves of lucent copper
yellow, scarlet and gold.
Looking up Farley noted a filagree of beech branch
forming intricate tracings against darkening cloud.
Shower in the offing?
He didn't mind, rain cleansed.
His gait on the carpet of fallen foliage became jauntier
he felt the caress of cool air,
rich in oxygen
on his hot face.

As he approached the river he heard the clamour of bird
peep, whistle, gobble, cluck
saw how silver willows
arched over the gleaming Avon
saw how silhouettes of duck, goose, gull and heron
reflected in the water beneath.
Between path and river, clusters of wrought iron seats
lined the bank and Farley now pleasantly fatigued
settled on a bench
near a wizened old man with hooked nose and straggly hair.
He pulled with arthritic finger
stale bread from plastic
all the while in high-pitched chirrup
calling to a gaggle of swans by the island.
Fascinated
Farley's mimic's mind revelled in the sounds
simultaneously observing the birds' raucous arrival.
They headed straight at him
massive wings spread
honking, treading water, splashing.
Farley felt like ducking but resisted
witnessing the turmoil and squabble
for a few bits of inedible bread.
The feast soon ended and the swans
now indifferent, formal, elegant
sailed back to their island.
Farley shifted attention to a student on neighbouring bench.
The lad scribbled assiduously and Farley seeing him surrounded
by balls of discarded paper
remembered Aldgate's advice.

Ever obedient he hauled out pen and pad
recording on countless page, word, sound and phrase.
Gaining in courage and momentum
he began creating fragments of repartee
in which each of his companions
gabbed away on different levels
gybing and weaving their blether into surprising new textures.
He tailored the roles
of course
to Aldgate and Farley
while the form loosely resembled
Samuel Beckett's 'Waiting for Godot."
Jotting down the names of Beckett's protagonists
Vladimir and Estragon
Farley burst into huge and glorious laughter.
He'd remembered
off the bat
without second thought
the data that eluded
him earlier.
Hurrah, he was cured!
Redemptive retirement assured.

Truncated

At the Norfolk County Fair
on a sunny afternoon in October
Felipe is disgruntled
wants candy, wants to go on the rides
wanted to stay longer with the reptiles
above all
as a boy
doesn't want to be in the women's washroom.
Outside the cubicle door
waiting for Mama as instructed
resentment seethes.
He senses Mama's at a disadvantage
decides to use it.
He checks her legs under the cubicle door
they're as sturdy as trees
growing from white sock and sensible lace-up.
They're not moving so he bolts out the door
barging his way through crowds in the passage
down the ramp, into the open.
Free at last!
He stops to listen for Mama's yell
checks to see if she following.
She's not.
His arms windmilling, bending this way and that,
he zigzags a circuitous route round a couple of booths
ending as intended with the reptiles.
Nose and hands pressed to smutty glass
he oohs at a coiled python, muscles rippling beneath shiny scale

aahs at a big white boa
adorned with faint orange diamonds
laughs at eyes opening vertically like curtains
squeaks in pleasure
at fleshy, purple, sausage-like appendages
that flop haphazardly along the spine of a giant lizard.
Then someone taps him on the shoulder
speaks.
He's a foreign child
has no English
turns and runs scampering off toward the livestock
his favourites.
On the way he darts about amongst the rides
keeping an eye open for Mama
determined to squeeze each last drop from his freedom.
Once in the building he squeals in delight
at familiar sound and sight.
He's attracted most
to the piglets, grunting and oinking,
as they suckle their mother.
He's hungry
would like to join them
but feels uneasy amongst strangers.
Instead he heads for a cow with a nice big udder.
A girl with a bucket spots him
shouts
so he's off again
this time to the horses.
He adores horses
they don't scare him, not one bit.
The barn is cavernous and wide
with the animals in open-ended stall on either side.

Unlike at home
they face their food and not the viewer.
That's not right
he likes to see the front
not the rump
but he's nothing if not adventurous
heads for a bay with hooves like platters.
Right away there's a yell, so he's off again as fast as a fish.
The poultry barn's next on his list
there he's greeted with pungent smells
and a deafening amalgam
of squawk, quack and peep.
It's bliss to his senses.
He sees a hen plucking her chest
knows its for her nest
sees through bar and netting
pigeons with tufted feet, and a haughty goose
glaring from a straight-lidded eye
rimmed in orange
to match a nostril in beak of milky glass.

He's finally slowing, starting to tire.
Now when he looks for Mama
he's hoping to find her, not dodge her.
He moves on to Produce, the sunflowers huge
pumpkins obese and sprawling.
They no longer hold his attention
he wants Mama
stumbles into the petting zoo
where a woman offers him a big white rabbit,
floppy ears and pink nose.
He cuddles the creature, hugs it to his chest.

It nuzzles, he likes it
squeezes tighter
too tight.
The woman speaks sharply
he drops the bunny
runs.
Where to?
Now dark, the lights are bright and glaring.
Shadows lurk between the stalls
disembodied, threatening.
A younger more boisterous crowd,
less solicitous of a child on his own,
mills about him.
Smells of food tease his senses
fries, popcorn, hamburger and sausage.
He needs food.
Where's Mama?
Again he scans the crowd
thinks he sees her entering a building
forces his way through legs
to find himself in unaccustomed setting
looming space divided by countless screen
no sign of Mama.
Bewildered he stands alone
a tiny figure with people flowing past
like water round a stone.

A woman watches from behind a screen raised on metallic legs
a foreign woman with black kerchief and bulging belly
In the crowd she sees the boy
her son
sees his pinched face
sees his black eyes searching
yet remains in hiding.
In this rich country
full of good, kind, responsible people
no harm can come to her child.
He's made for better things than she
pregnant, broke, rejected
can offer.
She bites on trembling lip
and as Felipe suddenly starts to approach
slips away.

Through the forest of legs Felipe sees
beneath a screen
a pair of legs that match his need
as sturdy as trees they grow from white sock and lace-up.
He tries to elbow his way
but first his path is blocked
then she's no longer there.
Lifting his eyes he sees her at the exit
wants to yell but no sound comes.
Frantic he shoves and pushes
reaches the door
too late.

It's now cold as well as dark.
In thin summer clothing he knows
he has get out of the wind.
Amidst blaring of loud-speaker, announcement and music
he hears the sound of a whinny,
follows the call
finds an enclosure offering rides on ponies.
He tries to scramble through ropes
but someone shouts and grabs his shirt.

At that moment something dies inside him.
Like a rabbit caught by the ears, he hangs limply in the man's grip.
The confident, rumbustious, mischievous Felipe
is lost forever.
His arms never again wind-mill
his mouth no longer forms words
his brain is a mass of raw pulsating terror
nothing else exists.

No one claimed Felipe.
He became Jake
living with Henrick and Betty
on a farm near Norwich.
They doted on him
giving him everything a child could want
yet he remained passive
never fully responding.
He seemed to start understanding English
yet never spoke
neither English nor any other language.

One evening near Thanksgiving
Jake in bed
his foster parents sat by open hearth
exchanging notes for the day.
"Jake's been with us a year," said Betty
knitting needles clacking.
Henrik, a man of few words, puffed on his pipe
didn't comment.
"A darling child," she continued, "beautiful
fair skin, dark hair, black eyes
must be of ethnic origin but which ethnicity?
Strange
that he never talks, laughs, smiles or cries.
Why?
What could have happened?
Where are his parents?
Such ambiguity.
How unlock his secrets?
Will he ever speak?"
Henrick, who tended Jake outdoors,
knew more of the child's true essence.
"We might never know for sure
yet his conduct tells us he's from rural back-ground."
"How would you know that?"
"He communes with animals
drinks from cows, snuggles with horses."
Betty who knew nothing of this
spluttered,

"That's dangerous, unhygienic!"
"Possibly, but it is his need
animals sense it, treat him as their own.
I've noted too he chooses wisely
judging each animal for mood and disposition."
Betty is doubtful: "A child so young?"
"It's instinct, not reason. He is gifted with senses
that we as humans
most likely possessed but do no longer."
Betty with little patience for what she considered esoteric
changed the subject,
"Henrick, you told me tomorrow
you have matters to attend at the fair,"
—it was again in full swing—
"perhaps Jake and I should accompany you.
He might enjoy it. Probably doesn't remember last year."

Once there
Betty held on to Jake's hand with fierce determination
but when in order to pay for candy
she let go
only briefly
he gave her the slip.

Jake had no plan
but guided by vague memories
located the women's washroom
then followed the route past reptiles, rides and poultry.
At the sight of the cows the customary need assailed him
but because of the crowds
he resisted
moving to the horses where the cavernous barn
matched his memories.
He sat on the floor near a bale of straw
checking his surroundings.
There was no one around
except in the mist at the end of the barn
against the light
a man on a ladder braiding the mane of a carthorse.
The smell of horse and hay
the sound of animals snorting and stamping
swishing their tails
comforted him.
Yet the horses themselves worried him
bigger, sleeker, more restless
than the sway-backed ponies he knew.
Also they faced away from him
all rump, no head
making appraisal impossible.
He saw one had a braided tail
another wore partial harness
but this didn't help in choosing.

He also wanted a horse that lay on the ground
all were standing.
His need was great, but with so much agin
he felt he should wait.
Then, as luck would have it,
close at hand
a chestnut folded long lean leg and settled.
Gleefully Jake abandoned his seat on the floor
joined the horse in the stall.

When Betty
frantic
arrived at the stables
all was confusion
siren, flashing light, ambulance.
a child, her child
lay on the ground on a stretcher
"My baby! My Jake," she sobbed trying to reach him
They held her back, "Madam, please . . ."
Jake's eyelids fluttered.
Turning his head
he saw legs, lots of legs.
None grew like tree-trunks from white sock and lace-up
yet in his mind
he saw these things with crystalline clarity
and before shutting his eyes
for good
said, "Mama."
Betty let out a howl for he'd never spoken
let alone called her Mama.

Persian Rug

Amir owns a cupboard of a store on Germain
where maritime rain and fog settle into joint and frizz hair
but not Amir's
for he's a Zoroastrian of ancient Persian lineage
with hair as heavy as the carpets he sells.
"See this one," he says, showing a rug from Tabriz.
"It's the goldfish pattern. Mahi"
—difficult for western ear.
I try it on the tongue: Mahi from Tabriz.
repeat, get it right and then look for fish
difficult for western eye.
He's patient
wants me to understand
explains
"Ah, yes, an abstraction," I say.
He's encouraged, gathers speed.
Flipping through the stack
he tells of machine-placed tuft
not right
and glory be
of proper knotting and counts per raj.
I begin to recognize the different looks and textures
seventy five is dense and fine, less is coarser.
Yet more voluble
he shows this motif and that
medallion from Isphahan
diamond from Kasham
Floral from Mashad.

My favourite's the dome
in browns, light blues and creams
alas, nine thousand dollars is not within my means
nor the Heriz
pattern of antique designer.
Amir continues undeterred.
the stacks reach high
so much to tell, so much to teach
here a Varamin
the pile's of wool
warp and weft of cotton
one sees it on the fringe.
If all is wool
sheep, goat or camel
the rug's stronger
withstanding hoof, sand, even man.
Silk's softer but good for highlight
see how luminous, how vibrant.
The torrent rolls on unabated
he speaks of natural dyes
of colour
and on a rug from Qum
points out a tone
named for desert flower
which for lack of rain blooms only rarely.
He doesn't know the English name
mustard I suggest but sand is more apt
for this scholar from the desert.
I'm listening to a quote from Persian poet
when sirens howl outside the door.

Transfixed we stare
as cruisers screech to grinding halt
police in combat gear, weapons drawn and ready
crash the entrance.
There's shouting, confusion, chaos
I'm pushed aside
land in rugs, dazed, at a loss to know what's happened.
I raise my head and see Amir
face down
handcuffed on the ground.
Police swarm like agitated ants ripping at carpet, wall and wire.
I see ill-bred people mishandling this man of letters
I see them yank him to his feet
his face as pale as a desert flower.
Gathering my senses yell,
"Stop! Terrible mistake.
This man's a teacher, scholar
let him be!"
But they're already on the street
stuffing Amir into jail.

What we did is wrong
Sorry, Amir, for what we've become.

The Veil

Friday night
bustling city mall
the young and beautiful are out in force
laptop, i-pod, blackberry, phone
all tinkle, beep and buzz, while friend greets friend
while long clean hair
swings to high-heeled stride.
At Holt's the tills jingle
instant tellers spit out the bucks
everywhere there's laughter
mirror
music
colour, noise and light.'
The western world's at play on Friday night.

At Starbucks
a girl appears in burka
tall, very tall
orders cream-topped mocha
settles in dark corner seat.
The mall falls silent, she's a threat
man in disguise?
bomb in garment?
What to do?
Sweat prickles, our hands go clammy
we're leery and full of fear.

Amidst sudden noise and laughter
a rowdy group draws closer.
They're young, cool, attractive
we feel like shouting
we're under threat
danger lurks in every corner
even here at Starbucks.

A blond boy with dread-locks and straight Greek nose
approaches
arms spread
he greets the mystery figure,
"You're here, Haleema! Awesome!"
With his help
the girl pulls off the burka
shakes loose lustrous curl
face exquisite
eyebrows plucked, lips a carmine red.
The body too is perfect
leg shapely, skirt short, heels high.
The boy busses painted cheek, saying
'We're going dancing, Haleema!"
She joins the noisy group and with them
saunters through the mall.

The next Friday
again we sit in Starbucks
again Haleema shows
orders cream topped Mocha
picks the selfsame spot.
The unprepared are fearful
leery
but we who know better are not.
Again the noisy group approaches
the blond boy spreads his arms
again he tugs away the burka.
There's a problem
he tugs and tugs some more
then suddenly from cotton fold
a face emerges
a man's face
fierce and bearded
the colour of cured tobacco.
A thunderous voice echoes through the mall
bouncing off ceiling, floor and wall
"Praise be to Allah! Allaaah! Allaaah!"
There's a scuffle
And . . . .

Simba Kubwa Speaks

You must realize I don't normally give interviews
but you're insistent
and we're a democratic society, so I'll spare you a few minutes.
I'm told you're interested in blood diamonds.
Intriguing!
I know nothing of such things and have never seen a red diamond.
I'd like one for my treasury.
Perhaps you can tell me, where might I acquire such an anomaly?

So you want to know about my treasury. It's like all treasuries
roomfuls of gold, silver, copper.
Jewels? Of course I have jewels! Rack upon rack of rubies, emeralds,
diamonds
I keep them in seamless sachets fashioned from buffalo scrotum.

You're right, stones help foot my tailors' bills
those crooks on Saville Row
sure know how to charge
but, as you say for this interview today
I chose something other than a suit
or, for that matter, other than the traditional clothing
I wore for China's envoy.
You probably saw the photos
fly-switch, sable-horn, tusk.
No?
I'm surprised. You missed something!

No!
I won't listen to what your saying.
You keep changing the subject and interrupting
it's bad manners.
I was telling you about my outfit and will continue.
For you
I've chosen this dressing gown from Benito's in Rome.
As you see, it's inlaid with mirrors of polished silver
small batteries sewn into the lining
provide for the tasteful use of lighting.
Ingenious, don't you think?
This lion's pelt on which I now recline
is also a favourite
fangs polished, head intact, eyes bejewelled.
it's a beauty.
Killed the beast myself back in the eighties.

With a gun?
Gun! Don't make me laugh!
a spear, man, spear!
as behooves The Simba Kubwa, Lion of Lions.
What did you say? I can't believe it!
After the time and hospitality I've offered you and your motley crew
turds every single one of you
after my willingness to overlook your impudence
my lenience with your boorish manners!
The ingratitude! I'm speechless
wounded to the core.
Do you not know who I am?

How dare you infer my country starves
because I live thus?
You English are so naive and ignorant
Can't you understand
if I lived differently
my people would have no respect?
As to the torture, prison and slaughter of innocents
as you so naively phrase it
I assure you nothing was ever done
that was not necessary
absolutely necessary.
What do you people know about being a fugitive
in one's own country
for decades, no less
sleeping in thorn trees, eating centipede
fighting for freedom from colonial oppressor like yourself?
What do you know about ruling a turbulent country?
About imposing order?
Don't come whining to me about slaughtered babies
people starving to death
every death was necessary
is necessary.
Now you will leave.
The guards will accompany you to a destination of *my* choice.
The Simba Kubwa has spoken.